I Love You When
by Alicia McBride

For my boys,
Aiden & Riley

Proceeds from this book benefit:
Julia Caoilainn Adams
who is currently fighting a rare form of brain cancer.

Please view her story here:
JuliaAdamsCancerFund.org

I love you when you're happy,
I love you when you're sad,

I love you when you're cranky,
I love you when you're glad.

I love you when
you're salty,
I love you when
you're sweet,

I love you when
you're stinky,
And even have
'tinky feet!

I love you when you're hot,
I love you when you're cold,

I love you when you're young,
I'll love you when you're old.

I love you
when you're
hungry,
I love you
when you're
full,

I love you when you're lonely,
Even when you pull the wool.

I love you when you're ornery,
Even when you're fighting mad.

I love you
when you mess up,
I love you
when you fall,

I love you when you're trying,
Even when you take a while.

I love you when
you're dirty,
I love you when
you're clean,

1 2 3 4 5 6 7 8 9 10
11 12 13 14 15 16 17
18 19 20 21 22 23
24 25 26 27
28 29 30

I'll love you when you're thirty,
And when you're seventeen.

I love you when you're irritable,
And even when you wail.

I love you when
you're content,
I love you when
you play,

I love you when you're peaceful,
I love you when you stay all day.

I love you when you're silly,
I love you when you're serious,

I love you when you're you,
I love you when you rhyme,
I love you through and through,
I love you

all the time!

With love, light and gratitude.

JULIA'S FIGHT AGAINST RARE CANCER

In Loving Memory:
Julia's Grandfather and Guardian Angel
Brad Largent
who lost his fight to cancer just one day
before Julia was diagnosed
12/11/53 - 11/8/18

Julia and her dad, just weeks before we knew she was sick

Our happy
22 month old

JuliaAdamsCancerFund.org

Made in the USA
Lexington, KY
12 April 2019